The Silver Lining

by
Mary'Beth Brady-Buckley

Illustrations by Jasmine Mills

The Silver Lining

PUBLISHED BY ROSEBUDTREASURES PUBLISHING

PRINTED IN THE UNITED STATES OF AMERICA
This book is a work of fiction. Names, characters, places, and incidents either are products of the author's imagination or are used fictitiously. Any resemblance to actual persons, living or dead, events, or locales is entirely coincidental.

Library of Congress Control Number: 2020913024
ISBN-13: 978-1-7348884-0-9

Author's Photograph ~ Beth Boudreau
Book Design ~ Karen White

Visit the website: www.marybethbradybuckley.com

This book is dedicated to my parents, Bill and Doll Brady. They taught us that when the storms of life are upon us, to keep smiling...there are lessons to be learned in the Silver Lining!

xoxo

It's March and the days
are cold and long.

Our teachers say,
"Wash your hands while
singing the Birthday song."

Soon after that we are told,
"All the kids have to stay home."

We can't
go to school
or play sports,

XOXO

so we play on our
parents' phones.

Then Mom and Dad
have to stay home too,
so we watch the news
to see what we should do.

4

A virus is here
that can make people sick.

Staying at home is the medicine
that will do the trick!

All of us at home
is something so new!

We try not to be bored,
and find fun things to do.

We see people
wearing gloves and masks.

All of this is scary...
until we learn
the facts.

This virus can spread
with just a touch,

or if someone coughs
and we breathe in
too much.

8

Our teachers give lessons
online, which is really cool.
And we teach Nana and Gampie
how to use computer tools.

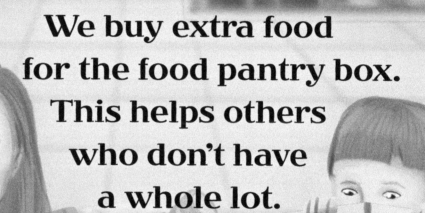

BREAD

CEREAL

SOUPS

BAKING

CHECK OUT →

We buy extra food
for the food pantry box.
This helps others
who don't have
a whole lot.

DONATE

Nana teaches us all
to cook and to sew,
and make delicious bread
from our rising dough!

She smiles and laughs,
and tells us not to worry.
"Let's enjoy this precious time,
when we don't need to hurry."

Gampie has his tools,
and we make leprechaun traps.

We get so
close to him,
suddenly we
are on his lap!

We go for long walks, sing, and jump over the cracks.

We check on our neighbors and bring them some snacks.

123

15

The days pass by, one by one.
Faster now that we are
having so much fun!

16

We sit by the fire, and Nana and
Gampie share their past.
They use old-fashioned words and
tell us how time goes by so fast.

They use crazy words like
bamboozle and persnickety,
then tell us to go and look them
up in our school dictionary!

Each night we pray for the sick and those caring for them.

And for the cashiers, janitors, volunteers, police, and firefighters... GOD BLESS all of them!

Being all together now is just like when they were young, they say.

Families home together, sharing stories back in their day!

"You see, kids," they tell us,
"life brings storms sometimes,
and we can't see the sun shining.
BUT if you look closely, listen,
and just wait...

you'll see
The
Silver
Lining!"

Old-Fashioned Words

Bamboozle   to trick or fool someone

Chum   a friend

Gander   to look or glance at something

Persnickety   to be fussy (about small details)

Shindig   a fancy party

Silver Lining   the good we can find, even in confusing, scary times!

My Favorite Memory of this time is...

_____

_____

_____

_____

_____

My name is _____

Date _____

Acknowledgements

Thank you to my family, Paul, Carley, and Ned for their continued support, input, and encouragement throughout this writing process. Thank you to my Mentor/Coach, Sandra Elaine Scott, for all of her words of wisdom, patience, and sense of humor, as she guided me into this new chapter of my life. Thank you to my Illustrator, Jasmine Mills, for listening closely and getting each character detail and theme of the book just right! Thank you to Karen White, my Book Designer, and my Editor, Susan Rooks, the Grammar Goddess, for polishing up *The Silver Lining*! It truly took a village!!

Above all, thank you, God, for all of your blessings and for opening up my eyes and heart, which allows me to always find The Silver Lining!

XO

CPSIA information can be obtained
at www.ICGtesting.com
Printed in the USA
LVHW071640230920
666052LV00072B/955